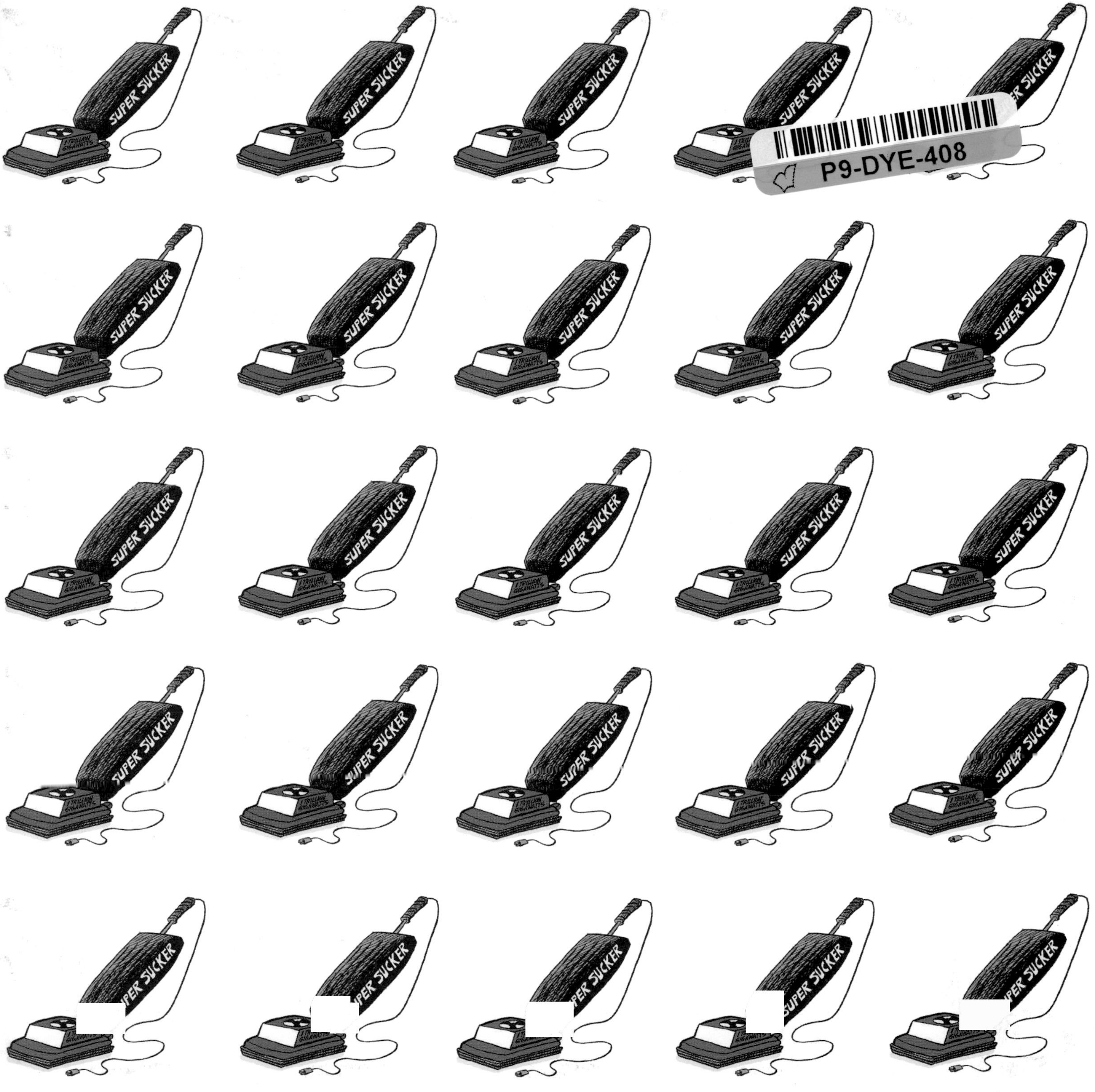

P9-DYE-408

BATTLE OF THE CHORES

Junior Discovers Debt

BY **DAVE RAMSEY**

ILLUSTRATED BY MARSHALL RAMSEY

DAVE RAMSEY'S JUNIOR'S adventures

Collect all of the Story Time Books!

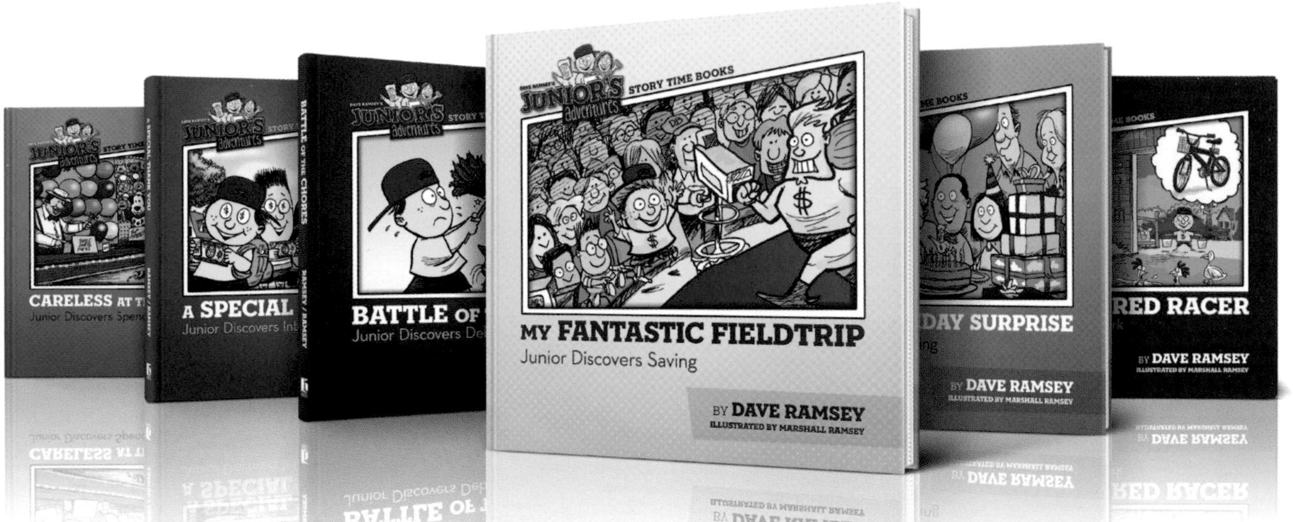

Battle of the Chores: Junior Discovers Debt
© 2012 Lampo Licensing, LLC
Published by Lampo Press, The Lampo Group, Inc.
Brentwood, TN 37027

All rights reserved. No portion of this book may be reproduced, stored in a retrieval system, or transmitted in any form or by any means—electronic, mechanical, photocopy, recording, scanning, or other—except for brief quotations in critical reviews or articles, without the prior written permission of the publisher.

For more information on Dave Ramsey, visit daveramsey.com or call 888.227.3223
For more information on Marshall Ramsey, visit www.clarionledger.com/ramsey

Editors: Amber Kever, Michele Christy, Debbie LoCurto, Darrin Dickey
Cover Design and Art Direction: Marshall Ramsey and Jason Miller
ISBN 978-0-9769630-1-1
12 13 14 15 [SGC] 5 4 3 2 1

DEDICATION

To Uncle Dave and Aunt Virginia—You've made an indelible mark on us.

As Marshall's parents and my namesake, you've exemplified a strong work ethic. You've ingrained in us the classic Ramsey way to live: Never pay too much.

Since it costs too much to pay interest on debt, we avoid debt, plain and simple.

We are grateful for your encouragement and love.

Dave (and Marshall)

"Nuh-uh," said Junior.

"Yuh-huh," said Rachel.

"Mom!" they yelled at the same time.

"Junior broke the head off my Darbie with his bulldozer!"

"It's not my fault that your doll jumped in front of my bulldozer!"

"You meant to do it!" said Rachel.

Mom entered the room and said, "Junior, as the older brother, you should set an example for your sister. Being a good example means you should not break her toys. Aren't you supposed to be cleaning your rooms right now?"

"Yes, ma'am," they replied.

Junior went to his room and looked around. He started putting his toys in his toybox. Then, he tossed his pillows back on his bed and pulled the covers up. He put his homework and books in his backpack and hung it over his desk chair.

Rachel went to her room and started to clean, but then she decided to play with her Sally Sweetheart doll. A few minutes later, Mom passed by her room and peeked in.

"Rachel, are you finished cleaning your room? It's time for dinner," said Mom.

"Almost. I've been decorating Sally Sweetheart's playhouse," said Rachel. "Do you like the stickers I put on her living room walls? Isn't her new hairdo pretty? Now, all I need is her **CELEBRATION** outfit." Rachel had seen a beautiful dress with a diamond necklace advertised at ALL-Mart.

"Yes, she's very pretty. Let's go eat dinner now," said Mom.

"Tomorrow is Saturday!" Junior announced at the dinner table. "It's my **FAVORITE** time because Dollar Bill's Adventures show is on TV!"

"Mom said that we are going to ALL-Mart! I will be able to get Sally Sweetheart's new **CELEBRATION** outfit!" said Rachel.

Junior and Rachel ran to the refrigerator to look at their Saving Charts.

"I hope I have enough money to buy my new DVD!" said Junior. "I've been saving my money **FOREVER**, but I spent some of it last weekend..."

"I should have enough money saved to buy Sally's **CELEBRATION** outfit. It looks like I've saved **ALL** my money since my birthday party," said Rachel.

They both ran to their rooms to get their **SAVE** and **SPEND** envelopes. Rachel pulled out her money. She counted and counted. "Twenty-five dollars!" she said. "Sally's **CELEBRATION** outfit is only twenty dollars!" Rachel put all of her money in her **SPEND** envelope. "I have enough to get Sally's outfit **AND** have money left over!"

Junior checked his envelopes, too. He opened up his **SPEND** envelope and it was **EMPTY!** He started to pout. Then, he looked in his **SAVE** envelope. "Only ten dollars?"

The next day at ALL-Mart, Mom got the shopping cart and headed to the food section. Junior and Rachel were so excited to get their toys; they could hardly keep from running through the store. Finally, they reached the **TOYS!**

"**YAY!** I'm going to get Sally's **CELEBRATION** outfit now!" said Rachel, running to the aisle with the dolls.

Junior ran to the DVD aisle and looked for the newest Dollar Bill DVD: Dollar Bill Escapes the Dreaded Dr. Debt! "Oh, no! It's fifteen dollars. I only have ten!" he moaned to himself.

Just then, Rachel came around the corner with Sally's outfit and saw Junior standing there with a sad look on his face.

"What's the matter, Junior?" she asked.

"I need five more dollars to get my DVD!" he said.

"Well, I have an extra five dollars that I can let you **BORROW** if you promise to pay me back."

"Oh, thanks, Rachel! You're the best little sister **EVER**! Sure, I'll pay you back!" said Junior.

Just then, Mom came around the corner and said, "Are you ready? Let's go!"

On the way home, Mom reminded them, “Please finish your chores **BEFORE** you play with your new toys.”

Junior headed outside to pick up his toys by the tree house and Rachel headed to the laundry room to fold a basket of towels. Rachel was so excited about Sally’s new outfit that she rushed to finish her chores. When she finished, she started rearranging Sally’s closet to make room for her new **CELEBRATION** outfit.

It was Junior's turn to do the dishes, so he rinsed the dishes and loaded them into the dishwasher. He filled it with most of the dishes from the sink, then stuffed in the rest. "Normal wash, heat dry," Junior said, as he pushed the buttons and turned on the dishwasher. It was late and Junior was not quite finished with his chores. He decided to go to bed early and finish his chores tomorrow.

Every Sunday, Junior and Rachel were paid for the chores they completed that week. After lunch, they gathered around their chore charts on the refrigerator. Mom asked what chores they finished yesterday. She put checkmarks by the chores written on the dry erase board.

Junior and Rachel pulled out their envelopes. Mom paid Rachel five dollars for finishing all of her chores this week. Rachel put one dollar in the **GIVE** envelope, two dollars in the **SAVE** envelope and two dollars in the **SPEND** envelope.

Junior only finished two of his chores this week. Mom paid him two dollars. He put one dollar in the **GIVE** envelope and one dollar in the **SPEND** envelope.

Rachel asked Junior, “Do you have the five dollars you owe me?”

“Well, I only have one dollar in my **SPEND** envelope, so that is all I can pay you today,” said Junior.

"Well," said Rachel, "when can you pay me the rest of my money?"

"Here's my dollar. I guess I'll pay the rest back in a few weeks," he said.

"A few weeks!" exclaimed Rachel. "I don't want to wait a few weeks! If you do some chores that are on **MY** list, you could pay me back next Sunday," said Rachel.

"Well, ok," he said.

"You can fold all the clothes this week, clean my room, and pick up my toys from around the house. That'll be three dollars. You still owe me one more dollar . . . you could do the dishes when it's my turn, too," she said.

"Rachel, that's a lot of work. Are you sure I can't just pay you back in a few weeks?" asked Junior.

"No. You owe me," she said.

"Ok, fine. I guess I will have to do your chores, too, since I **OWE** you the money," grumbled Junior. He wasn't very happy about this arrangement and began to doubt his decision to borrow money from Rachel.

After school on Monday, Junior started his chores. He took his clothes to the laundry room and started vacuuming the living room.

Rachel was sitting on the couch, playing with Sally Sweetheart and her new outfit. She reminded Junior, "Don't forget to do my chores, too, Junior. I need that money back."

"I know," said Junior, with a long face. He worked hard to finish his chores and start on Rachel's. He knew he had to get ALL the chores done. He **OWED** money to Rachel!

By the time he finished **ALL** the chores, he was **TIRED**. He went to his room, picked up his DVD, promised himself that he would watch it tomorrow, and then fell into bed.

When Junior and Rachel got home from school on Tuesday, Junior began his long list of chores. He finished folding the laundry from Monday night. He unloaded the dishwasher and put all the dishes away.

At dinner, Junior piled his plate high with food.

"Wow, Junior, you must be hungry!" said Dad. "Did you have a good day at school?"

"Yes, I beat Billy in the relay races!" replied Junior.

After dinner, Junior wanted to watch his **NEW** DVD. As he walked into the living room, Rachel said, “Don’t forget, Junior, you have to do **MY** chores, too, since you **BORROWED** my money.” So, he went outside and picked up Rachel’s toys. Then, he rinsed the dirty dishes and put them in the dishwasher. He spent the rest of the night doing her chores.

The next night, Junior thought, “Tonight, **SURELY**, I will watch my new DVD. I just **HAVE** to see how Dollar Bill escapes the dreaded Dr. Debt!”

Again, Rachel reminded him, “Junior, don’t forget to clean my room tonight. You owe me.” She went into the living room to watch TV and Junior sulked in his chair. He knew he wouldn’t be able to see how Dollar Bill escapes the dreaded Dr. Debt again tonight.

So, he gathered Rachel's socks and shoes, backpack and toys, and took them to her room. He put everything away, dusted, and vacuumed her bedroom.

When it was time for commercials, Rachel went to her room to get Sally Sweetheart.

"Don't forget to put **ALL** of my shoes on the rack in my closet," she said.

"Rachel, I am **TIRED** of doing all your chores," said Junior.

"But, you **OWE** me. If you don't pay me back, I'll tell Mom!" said Rachel.

"Okay, I'll finish your chores," said Junior, with a frown. He didn't want Mom to find out that he had borrowed money.

Rachel went back to the living room to watch TV.

Mom walked past Rachel's room and asked, "Junior, what are you doing in Rachel's room?"

"Well, I can't tell you, Mom," said Junior.

"What are you talking about?" asked Mom. "Where's Rachel?"

Before he could answer, Mom yelled, “Rachel! Come to your room. Explain to me why it appears that your brother is cleaning **YOUR** room?”

Junior and Rachel just stared at each other.

“Umm . . . well . . . ok, I let Junior borrow five dollars so he could get his DVD,” Rachel explained. “And I thought he could pay me back faster if he did my chores this week.”

"I see. So, Junior, was it worth it?" asked Mom.

"What do you mean?" asked Junior.

"I mean, was it worth it to be in **DEBT** to your sister in order to get your DVD?" asked Mom.

"NO. I haven't had time to play with any of my toys because I've been doing too many chores! I feel like her slave!" he said.

"Yes, well, Rachel, I appreciate that you were trying to help Junior, but we don't loan money in this family. When you **LOAN** money to someone, you change your relationship with them. Junior, in order to pay Rachel back, you did **ALL** of your chores and **ALL** of her chores—you weren't working for your **OWN** money, you were working for her," said Mom.

"I did **NOT** have fun this week," said Junior.

"Junior, what if you had saved your own money for one more week? You would have earned enough money to purchase your own DVD. You wouldn't have had to do twice the amount of chores this week," said Mom.

"I just didn't want to wait," said Junior.

"I see. Well, did you get to watch your DVD this week?" asked Mom.

"No, I haven't even unwrapped it. I was too busy doing chores!" said Junior. "I would have been happier if I'd waited. I wouldn't have worked so hard this week!"

Rachel felt bad for how she had treated Junior. "I'm sorry, Junior. I had no idea that letting you **BORROW** money would cause all this **TROUBLE!** I was just trying to help!"

"In the future, if you want to help someone, children, **GIVE** them the money. That way, you help them—instead of making them **OWE** you," explained Mom.

"That's a great idea, Mom! Hey, there is one job I wouldn't mind doing," said Junior. "To the kitchen—I'll make ice cream sundaes for everyone!"

They all laughed and headed to the kitchen for ice cream.

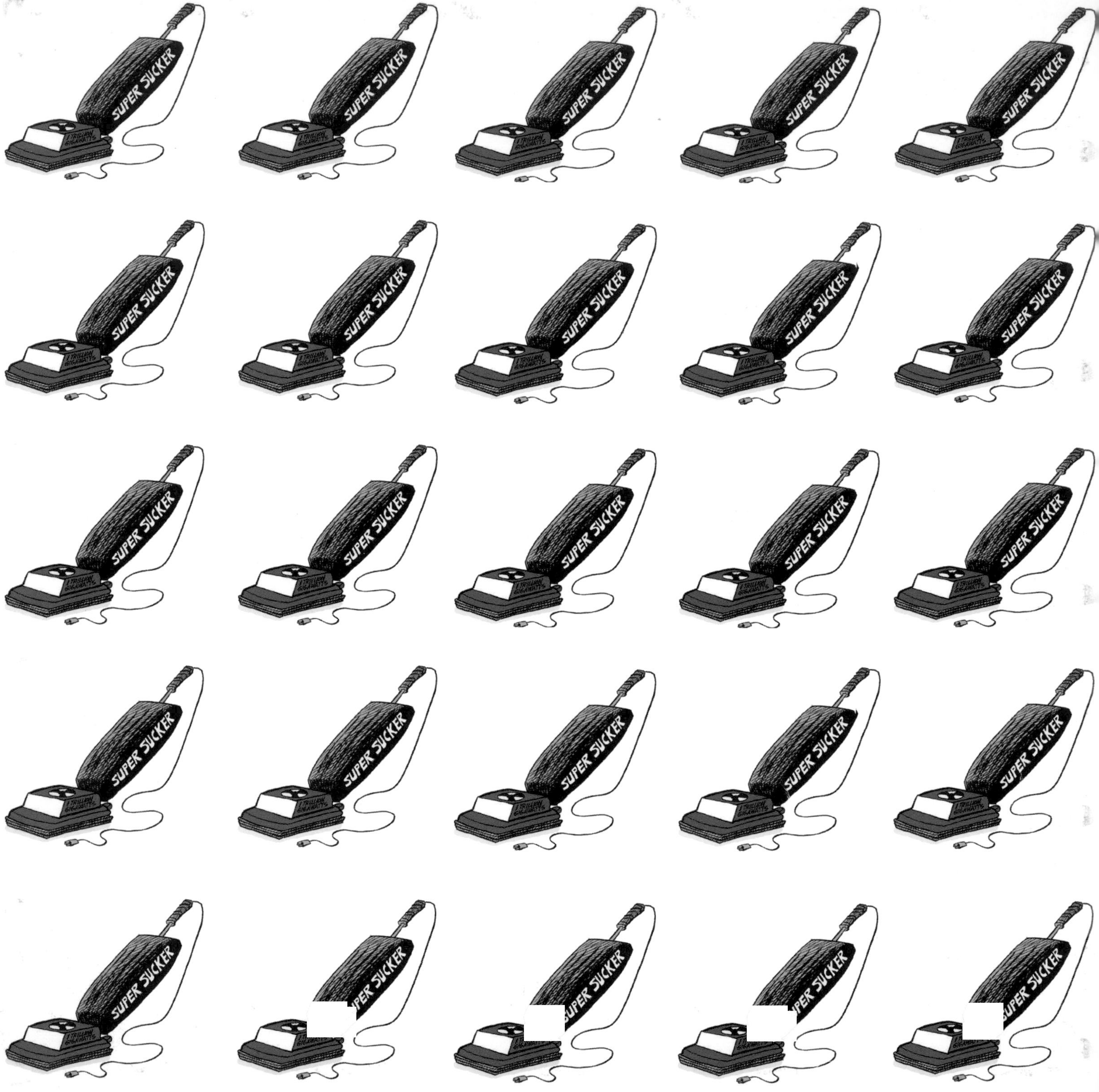
SUPER SUCKER
1 TRILLION GIGAWATTS